RAVEN & SNIPE

Anne Cameron

Illustrations by Gaye Hammond

HARBOUR PUBLISHIN

Harbour Publishing Co. Ltd.
Box 219, Madeira Park, BC
Canada V0N 2H0
Cover and book design by Gaye Hammond

Published with the assistance of the Canada Council

Reprinted June, 1992

Canadian Cataloguing in Publication Data

Cameron, Anne, 1938–
Raven and Snipe

ISBN 1-55017-037-6

1. Indians of North America–British Columbia–Pacific Coast–Legends–Juvenile literature. 2. Legends–British Columbia–Pacific Coast–Juvenile literature 3. Ravens–Folklore–Juvenile literature. I. Hammond, Gaye. II Title.
E78.N78C34 1990 j398.2′089′970711 C90-091604-4

When I was growing up on Vancouver Island I met a woman who was a storyteller. She shared many stories with me, and later gave me permission to share them with others.

This woman's name was KLOPINUM. In English her name means "Keeper of the River of Copper." It is to her this book is dedicated, and it is in the spirit of sharing, which she taught me, these stories were offered to all small children. I hope you will enjoy them as much as I did.

Anne Cameron

Raven is a glutton.

No matter how much she has to eat, Raven is always hungry. But rather than work to feed herself, Raven prefers to resort to trickery. As often as not her tricks backfire on her.

Raven spends much of her time on the beach, looking for food and trying to find ways to trick the other birds and animals into feeding her. One day she noticed that Snipe always seemed to have a good supply of food. Snipe and her husband were busy from the time the sun came up until after it went back down again, gathering and storing food.

Raven wanted some of Snipe's food.

She went to where Snipe and her husband lived and looked at what they had gathered, stored, and preserved. Clams, oysters, berries, nuts, and fish of all kinds were dried, smoked, salted, and carefully stored for times of need.

Raven wanted some of that food.

In fact, Raven wanted all of that food!

Raven knew as well as anybody the rules of hospitality. And she decided to use these rules for her own benefit. Raven walked boldly up to Snipe's house and knocked on the door. When Snipe opened the door, Raven smiled. "Hello," she said, "I've come to visit you and Mr. Snipe and the children."

"Come in," said Snipe, opening her door wide and stepping aside to allow Raven to enter.

"Hello Mr. Snipe," said Raven politely, her sharp eyes noticing how well fed he was. "Hello all you little Snipes," she smiled, noticing how shiny their feathers were, how bright their eyes. "My," she said, "something in here smells good."

"Would you join us for supper?" Snipe asked, knowing full well Raven never said no to a free meal.

Raven smiled and nodded, and they all sat down to share food. "Thank you," the little Snipes said when their mother gave them their supper. "Thank you," said Mr. Snipe. "Thank you," said Raven. Then, while the others ate their meal quietly and politely, Raven started to feed herself. She gobbled and belched, she stuffed her beak and talked with her mouth full, she slobbered and drooled and reached with both hands, she picked up food with her fingers, she did everything except get her feet in the meal.

The Snipes could not believe what they were seeing.

Raven chomped and snoffled, she munched and burped, she smacked her lips and slurped and kept reaching for more, more, more.

Snipe realized Raven had no intention of leaving until every scrap of food was gone.

"We're very fortunate," Snipe said quietly, "we always have an abundance of food."

"Yes," Raven belched, reaching for more.

"It's because my mother was a magic woman," Snipe confided. "A shaman who knew many mysteries."

"Really?" Raven slowed down, but she did not stop eating and gorping.

"Oh, yes," Snipe smiled. "Any time it looks as if we're running out of food, I just have to do some of the magic my mother taught me and we have more of everything."

"Really?" Raven was fascinated. "I don't suppose," she said with her mouth full, "there would be any way a person could talk you into sharing some of what your mother taught you."

"Oh, of course," Snipe smiled. "I'd be delighted. But I can't do the magic in the house, we have to go outside for that."

In a flash, Raven was away from the table, out of the house, and outside, waiting greedily to learn how to have an unlimited supply of food without ever having to do any work at all.

Snipe and her family went outside, carefully closing and locking the door so Raven could not get back inside to devour every scrap and morsel.

"First I'll light a fire," Snipe said. "Everybody gather up some dry wood so I can do my magic."

Raven raced around gathering wood, and, since she didn't know how big the fire had to be, she gathered all the wood she could find and piled it near Snipe's house. There was enough firewood there for months and months. The Snipe children smiled happily because it was their job to make sure there was always enough wood, and now Raven, without knowing it, had done much of the work for them.

"When the fire is going," Snipe explained, "I have to dance through it four times. But nobody is to watch me do this. So while I am dancing, you have to keep your eyes shut, and concentrate."

Raven closed her eyes and concentrated. She thought of mountains of smoked salmon, piles of huckleberries and blackberries, mounds and heaps of nuts, and stacks and piles of oysters and clams.

"I'm dancing through the fire now," Snipe sang. But she only danced around it, and bent over to pick up some cool ashes to rub them on her feet and legs to make it look as if she had, in fact, danced in the fire.

She danced over to a log and pulled off a handful of soft moss. "I'm looking for a stone," she sang, "a sharp sharp stone, the sharper the better."

She danced over to where she had a secret stockpile of fish eggs, took a double handful of the fish eggs, and hid them inside the moss.

"You can open your eyes now, if you want," she said. Raven opened her eyes.

Snipe was dancing on the other side of the fire, and Raven couldn't see very clearly because of the bright light in her eyes. She squinted and peered, and through the smoke and the sparks saw Snipe with what looked like a very sharp, very pointed stone in her hand.

"I have to bang myself on the leg," Snipe explained. "I have to do it six times to complete the magic," and six times she raised the handful of moss filled with fish eggs, and brought it against her leg. Each time the moss touched her leg, she clacked her beak together, making a sound that convinced Raven Snipe really was bashing herself on the leg.

"Magic!" Snipe laughed, dropping the moss and lifting from it the double handful of fish eggs.

"Here," she handed the eggs to Raven who gobbled them down immediately.

"Would you teach me?" Raven asked, thinking that with this trick she would never again have to worry about food.

"Close your eyes," Snipe advised, and Raven closed her eyes. "Now dance," Snipe commanded.

Raven began to dance.

"Dance where I lead you," Snipe said, and Raven obeyed.

Snipe danced Raven to the edge of the fire, and then pointed Raven at the fire. "Dance forward," Snipe said, and Raven danced into the fire.

"Ow!" Raven screeched.

"Keep dancing!" Snipe called. "You have to remember this is Magic!"

Raven danced and hopped and squacked and yelled with pain and finally danced herself out of the fire.

"Turn around and come back," Snipe said, "you have to dance in the fire four times."

Raven wasn't feeling very enthusiastic about any of this, but she remembered all the food Snipe had, food Snipe said came from magic, and Raven, above all else, is a glutton.

She danced back into the fire, burning her legs and feet, singeing her feathers, cawing loudly in pain.

"Now the rock," Snipe said, choosing the biggest, heaviest, sharpest rock she could find. "Strike yourself on the leg as hard as you can; if it isn't done right, you won't get any food."

Raven took the rock, swung it as hard as she could, and bashed herself on the ankle.

"Ouch!" she screamed.

"You'll have to do it again," Snipe said, almost laughing out loud. "You couldn't have done it hard enough because nothing happened."

"NO!" Raven yelled, weeping. "There has to be a better way to get food than this! I'm not doing this again, it isn't worth it!" and she ran away, crying bitterly.

The Snipes went back to work collecting, gathering, preserving, and storing food, making happy little noises as they worked, stopping often to remember how foolish Raven had been in her gluttony. And if, when you go to the beach, you move slowly and quietly, and find a comfortable place to sit, then sit very still and very quiet, Snipe and her family will begin to trust you, and you will be able to hear the happy noises they make as they work.

You may even hear Raven as she complains and protests enviously. But you will notice she never bothers the Snipes as they work.

OTHER BOOKS BY ANNE CAMERON

FOR CHILDREN

How Raven Freed the Moon	$4.95	paper
How the Loon Lost Her Voice	$4.95	paper
Orca's Song	$4.95	paper
Raven Returns the Water	$4.95	paper
Spider Woman	$4.95	paper
Lazy Boy	$4.95	paper
Raven Goes Berrypicking	$5.95	paper

FOR ADULTS

Earth Witch (poetry)	$5.95	paper
The Annie Poems (poetry)	$7.95	paper
Dzelarhons (legends)	$8.95	paper
Stubby Amberchuk & the Holy Grail (novel)	$19.95	cloth
Women, Kids & Huckleberry Wine (short stories)	$12.95	paper
Tales of the Cairds (legends)	$9.95	paper
South of an Unnamed Creek (novel)	$19.95	cloth
Bright's Crossing (short stories)	$12.95	paper
Escape to Beulah (novel)	$14.95	paper
Kick the Can (novel)	$14.95	paper